D0527698

S

FIRE
BELL
S
S

S
S

JONATHAN CAPE

UK | USA | Canada | Ireland | Australia
India | New Zealand | South Africa

Jonathan Cape is part of the Penguin Random House group of companies
whose addresses can be found at global.penguinrandomhouse.com.

www.penguin.co.uk www.puffin.co.uk www.ladybird.co.uk

First published 2020
001

Printed in Malaysia
A CIP catalogue record for this book is available from the British Library

ISBN: 978–0–857–55117–7

All correspondence to:
Jonathan Cape, Penguin Random House Children's
One Embassy Gardens, New Union Square
5 Nine Elms Lane, London SW8 5DA

Stanley's
Fire Engine

JONATHAN CAPE • LONDON

It's going to be another busy day at Stanley's Fire Station.

FIRE STATION
KEEP CLEAR

Stanley and Peggy keep Stanley's fire engine in tip-top condition.

It needs to be ready for anything!

Stanley's
fire
engine
has
very
long
ladders
so
he
can
reach
very
high
places . . .

. . . like the tops of trees when
kites and teddies and Little Woos
get stuck up them.

FIRE

Stanley's fire engine also has VERY long hoses.

They're perfect for extinguishing Charlie's annual barbecue . . .

. . . or cooling down anyone feeling hot and bothered.

CLANG! CLANG! CLANG! goes the bell . . .

which means “GET OUT OF THE WAY!”

We're going to the FIREWORKS!
Stanley and Peggy are standing by
in case of accidents.

But Shamus and Hattie know what they are doing, so everything goes off with . . .

. . . a bang, a whizz, a swoosh and a KABOOM!

Well! What a busy day!

Stanley's House

Time for tea!

Time for a bath!

S

And time for bed!
Goodnight, Stanley.